Quiet STORM

VOICES OF YOUNG BLACK POETS

Selected by

Lydia Omolola Okutoro

JUMP AT THE SUN
Hyperion Books for Children

First Edition
1 3 5 7 9 10 8 6 4 2
This book is set in 11/14-point Garamond.

Library of Congress Cataloging-in-Publication Data
Quiet Storm/edited by Lydia Omolola Okuturo.
p. cm.
ISBN 0-7868-0461-0
1. Young adult poetry, American-Afro-American authors. 2. Afro-Americans-Poetry.
[1. American poetry-Afro-American authors-Collections. 2. Poetry-Black authors-
Collections. 3. Afro-Americans-Poetry. 4. Blacks-Poetry. 5. Youths' writings.] I.
Okutoro, Lydia.
PS591.N4Q85 1999
811.008'0896-dc21 98-30346

iv

For both of my families:

the Okutoro Family, who was brave enough
to let a daughter and sister go so far away from home,

and the Perkins Family, who was brave enough
to adopt a daughter and sister into their home.

And for Nana, who became my bridge.

v

CONTENTS

WEARING OUR PRIDE
Poems about Black Pride, Unity, and Beauty

• •

WE, THE OBSERVERS
Poems about the Poet as Keeper of the Oral Tradition

• •

MOTHERLANDS ‘AND THE HOOD

Poems about Home and "Homelessness"

• •

TRIP TO MY SOUL
Poems that Reflect on Self and Spirit

• •

x

Love Rhythms
Poems about Falling in Love and the Music it Brings

● ●

THE STRUGGLE CONTINUES
Poems about the Fight for Freedom

• •

YOUT REBELS /Linton Kwesi Johnson 59

After Tomorrow
Poems about Hopes and Dreams of a Brighter Future

TO OUR ELDERS
Poems that Salute Ancestors, Elders, and Mentors

· ·

WINDOW MORNING / Mwatabu S. Okantah 77

TALKING DRUMS #1
for the poets

Carved from that same tree
in another age
counsel/warriors
who in the mother tongue
made drums talk
now in another tongue
make words to walk in rhythm
'cross the printed page
carved from that same tree
in another age.

—Khephra Burns

SPECIAL THANKS

Quiet Storm: Voices of Young Black Poets began as a dream when I was a high school student at St. Paul's School in Concord, New Hampshire. I was able to hold onto and nurture that dream from its conception, with the help of my families, many friends, and various others whom God allowed to cross my path. So, I give thanks to that force we call God for giving me the dream, for blessing me with two families—one Nigerian, one American—both of whom I love dearly, and for putting positive and loving friends in my life.

Mommy, wherever you are, God bless you and keep you safe. Daddy, I thank you for your quiet strength and amazing patience. Harold, thank you for being an example that fathers, too, can be nurturing. Patty, I cannot even begin to thank you for being my mother. I hope you both know that I appreciate all your love and sacrifices. To my brothers and sisters—Moses, Jonathan, Kayode, Bisayo, Shawnice, Donnya, Jaye—I have nothing but love for you all. Tyrell and Ciara, this is for you, too. You are the future. Much love to you, Grandma Perkins. And I cannot forget Nana, who, many years ago, took a young Yoruba girl into her home and made her a daughter and then a granddaughter. Nana, I love you, and I thank you.

To my friends who have been on this great journey with me, I hope we have many more together. Taisha Lewis, Shamina Sneed, Simisola Sanni: Let the world remember these names, they'll be taking over someday! Many thanks to my *Essence* family: Corliss Hill (Big Sis); Tara Roberts, for giving me the connections; Angela Kinamore, for being there at the conception of the dream and thereafter; and Susan L. Taylor, for the words of wisdom and inspiration.

Much love to my sisters from Mount Holyoke College. MHACASA and APAU, you know who you are. Long live the sisterhood! Special thanks to my "committee" of friends, teacher-mentors, and helpers. Simi, Sabine Thomas, Phillippa Thiuri, Li-May Hor, Anita Henderson, Sherri Vanden Akker, John Lemly: Your critiques helped more than you know. To the countless others who are not mentioned here, know that it is not because I have forgotten. Thank you for giving of yourselves even when I thought myself too independent to ask.

I am immensely grateful to my editor, Andrea Davis Pinkney. Thanks for believing in my work and taking it on. Thanks also to Mike Conathan. To all the young poets who answered the call for this book from across the United States, Canada, and England, thank you for keeping the tradition alive. *Quiet Storm* would not have been possible without you.

—L. O.

INTRODUCTION

I was born in Nigeria, and I have lived in the United States since moving here when I was nine years old. When I came here in the summer of 1983, I felt almost immediately like an outcast. My hair was short and natural (before it became vogue); my clothes were traditional Nigerian styles. I was ashamed of these things that separated me from American kids, so I abandoned them. Eventually I lost my telltale foreign accent and my language, Yoruba.

But I am going through a new transformation. Like many African Americans, I am "returning to my roots." One of the ways I do this is through poetry that is rooted in African tradition. When I was a student at St. Paul's School in Concord, New Hampshire, I edited a small collection of writings and artwork by students and alumni of that high school. The idea for *Quiet Storm: Voices of Young Black Poets* came out of that experience, which inspired me to do a similar project on a large scale. A few of the poems here were in that first collection.

We young people read and get inspired by the poetry of Langston Hughes, Maya Angelou, Nikki Giovanni, Noemia de Sousa, Linton Kwesi Johnson, Mwatabu Okantah, Lucille Clifton, and Alexis De Veaux—the wonderful poets whose works open each themed section of this book. *Quiet Storm* is a celebration of the African Diaspora through *our* eyes. It is a way for us to inspire and teach one another.

Until recently, that word, "Diaspora," had only been associated with Jews because of their dispersion from Israel. Therefore, it had only religious connotations. However, in the past few years, Diaspora has come to indicate the cultures of

African-descended people who can be found in almost all the countries of the world. The African Diaspora—which is an extension of the African continent—refers to the West Indies, Central and South America, the United States, Canada, Europe, and anywhere else that African peoples make their home.

Diaspora suggests not only a common ancestry of African people throughout the world, but also their shared experiences and ways of responding to their situations. In the same way, "Black" refers to any person of color with African heritage. The "Black Experience" does not only belong to African Americans. It means being West Indian, Haitian, or Panamanian; it means being a Nigerian living in the United States or England; it means being a Senegalese living in France; it means being of St. Vincent parentage and living in Canada. The sixty-one poems in *Quiet Storm* celebrate this awareness of parallel cultures while acknowledging a common—if distant—heritage.

The call for poetry to be included in this book brought in over eight hundred poems from all over Canada, England, and the United States. Some of the poets are from Jamaica, Haiti, Barbados, Panama, Nigeria, Somalia, St. Thomas, Zaire, and Uganda. Such an overwhelming response to this project is evidence that a forum such as this for our creative voices needs to happen more often. The forty-nine young poets here wrote their poems at the ages shown. They represent only a sampling of the powerful oral tradition, a tradition that needs to be nurtured and continued.

—LYDIA OMOLOLA OKUTORO

STORM QUIET

WEARING OUR PRIDE

Poems about Black Pride, Unity, and Beauty

● ●

MY PEOPLE

The night is beautiful
So the faces of my people.
The stars are beautiful,
So the eyes of my people.
Beautiful, also, is the sun.
Beautiful, also, are the souls of my people.

—Langston Hughes

QUIET STORM
(for my ebony people)

As a generation of
ebony people
struggle to return
to their roots,
reaffirm their places in the sun,
and renew their identities with
The Motherland,
I listen.
it's in the names of the children,
and the song-languages:
Swahili, Yoruba, Hausa.
it's in the sense of pride
befitting kings and queens.
And I
a full-blooded ebony AFRICANA,
born to Lagos, Nigeria
(AFRICA, to be exact)
enter
and join the struggle
calmly
like a Quiet Storm.

—LYDIA OKUTORO, 18
   Nigeria

MY BLACK SELF

What do you prefer to be called?
Negro . . .
Colored . . .
African American . . .
Pan-African . . .

Our name should measure up to who
we are
where we've been
what we go through
and what our future holds.

So I prefer to be black
Just plain black will suffice.
It needs no sprucing up.

I am a magnificent spectrum of color.
A glorious interpretation of all that
molds my heritage.
No lighter . . . no better
No darker . . . no worse
Just plain black.

I am my native land. My beauty is like
the African violet.
My emotions flow as deep as the rolling
indigo rivers of West Africa
that rescued my people from slavery's
clutches.
The green you see in my eyes—and call
envy—it is just that,

but not for what you think.
It is merely a reflection from your own
jealousy.
You long to be like me.

My aura glows as golden yellow as the
sweltering sun
that beat down on my ancestors in the
fields.
And my blood abounds as rich as any
red-blooded native
of the nation.
My skin can be orange, my eyes can be
blue . . .
no shade defines me
no shade defines you.

We are beauty. Beauty is what we see.
No darker . . . no better.
No lighter . . . no worse.
Just plain black.

—KATRICE L. MINES, 18
   Ohio

MESSAGE TO THE DARK-SKINNED IN DENIAL

YOU CAN'T HIDE IT
Your darkness screams
through your skin.
As dark as crisp charcoal
smoking on a grill.
As dark as a hole escaping to
an endless end.
As dark as all the Black
people ever swallowed
by the streets.

You're the deepest deep there ever
could be,
and I love your darkness.

I STAND NEXT TO YOU
And wish your darkness
would kiss my skin
And send me those secret
sugary songs, seeping
slowly from not Tan, not
Brown, but melted Fudge skin.

I STAND NEXT TO YOU
And take journeys through
your eyes
Traveling your roads of
rejection
I see my history lined in
your lips

You are dark
and ooh, you are the slick,
deep shade that has
sophisticated shyer hues
You are the groovy booming beat in
shaky bass blues

You are Black bending all boundaries
You are Black diving beyond dangerous
depths
You are Black captured
centerpoint
in All eyes.

—CHRISANDRA C. WELLS, 18
Nebraska

NAPPY HEAD

These dancing spirals
  around my head
twist and kink
    curling
frizzingly at the ends
into a shiny halo
of beautiful African hair.

And you call it nappy?

—MARIA GALATI, 18
  Wisconsin

MY FIRST LOVE

My first love be
Hair
natural
ain't washed for weeks
Hair
the myrrh and the musk of it
Hair
the lilac blossomin'
of ancient shrubbery
Hair
parted by rivers
of grease and kink
Hair
a plantation of jujubes
cultivated by tender hands
Hair
agitated to tremblin' bliss
Hair
unruly comb-breakin'
Hair
burstin' hematite and obsidian aglow
Hair
eternal smokin' afro bush
with a black power fist
raised like a pyramid
Hair
outta control forest fire
approachin'
your city
Hair

that drifts
and grows
shamelessly
in touch with the deep-grown roots
of the fertile land
called scalp
Hair
she be my first love.

—JENNIFER MCLUNE, 18
  New York

HALO

The Lord,
She took her time–
To curl
every
strand
of my hair
to create
My Crown–
My Glory–
My Halo!

—KELLEY M. PAGE, 19
Massachusetts

MULATTO CHILD

"What is it like?"
Asked the child
With wide eyes full of innocence,
Windows picturing a world
Free of lines defining
Who someone is
By what she is.
I looked deep into those eyes
Dark as Grandmother's mahogany table.
I could not answer her.
I tried to express
All that is inexpressible in the soul.
The loneliness of the mixed thousands
Who have gone before me.
Words were not enough.
Their struggle to find a place in a society
Where they were the true outsiders.
Accepted by no one, fitting in
nowhere.
This is my heritage.
Born of the richness
Of two different ancestries
Combining to form one.
So when someone calls me a
MULATTO BITCH.
An OREO,
A ZEBRA,
Or some kind of
COOKIES 'N' CREAM mush,
I am not offended.
I consider it an honor.

A privilege to possess my heritage.
Those who insult my uniqueness
Only reveal their own ignorance
And an inability to have respect
for their own culture,
Let alone that of another.

So as I look into the eyes of the child
I simply observe the hopes, dreams,
Realities and fantasies of the
Entire world.
Building a new society
In the shining depths of her mahogany eyes.

—ELIZABETH G. WESTON, 17
New Jersey

HAIKUS FOR THE SISTERS

I. (For ShaShona)
　　With eyes like Egypt
　　And skin the color of Earth
　　She searches for Truth.

II. (For Shamina)
　　Stand and spread your wings
　　And on your rich cocoa skin
　　Wear your India.

III. (For Monique)
　　The love in her heart
　　Which is like the seeds of Spring
　　Sprouts her into being.

IV. (For Shanique)
　　If the Earth opens her arms
　　Embrace her. If she
　　Opens her ears, sing.

V. (For Taisha)
　　Carry the crystal
　　That is your life with ease
　　If it falls, pick up the pieces.

—LYDIA OKUTORO, 17
　　Nigeria

MUTT

When you see me
  Do you see
The color of Africa?
Do you see the rhythm of Cuba?
  Do you see
The strength of the Cherokee?
  Do you see
The empire of China?
  Do you see
The tropics of the Caribbean?
If not, look closer.

—ZARINAH JAMES, 16
  New York

WE, THE OBSERVERS

Poems about the Poet as Keeper of the Oral Tradition

I AM THE CREATIVITY

I am the dance step
of the paintbrush singing
I am the sculpture
of the song
the flame breath
of words
giving new life to paper
yes, I am the creativity
that never dies
I am the creativity
keeping my people alive

—Alexis De Veaux

I WRITE POEMS

I write poems
Like the ocean.
My pen
More regular,
More everlasting
Than the tide
Sweeping my white beaches
With a current of purpose
I write poems
Like the ocean.
Silver-black, joyful, soulful.
And just as powerful.

—ROCHELLE N. SPENCER, 17
   Georgia

IN SEARCH OF THE BEAT

Wanted to be a poet,
You know, the kind that
Could unravel sweet words while a
slow,
Constant, subtle, melodious beat
Engulfed the air.

Wanted to be a poet,
The kind whose words warmed,
Soothed, induced fits of passion,
While that faint beat continued.

Wanted to be a poet,
The kind that people revered,
Hated, enjoyed, were indifferent to
But the beat,
It didn't comply.

Wanted to be a poet,
The kind that could express
Many views on a whim
But my beat began to wane.

Wanted to be a poet,
The kind that wrote and
Revised and read and
Crumbled paper
While creating vibrant beats.

I wanted to be a poet,
But then you stole my tune
And told me that the
Beat
had died.

—DEBORAH Y. DE SHONG, 18
New York

JAM WITH A POET & DANCER

i wanted to dance
  my words
  when i was young
i wanted my words
    to dance
  in r&b, in love,
    in my anger
i wanted to dance
  so that mommy could get healthy
  so that daddy could come live with us
  so that i could rest from all instructions
i wanted to dance
        superbly
          phenomenally
            & in supreme worship
you see,
i wanted to dance
so bad that i became a poet
at heart,
  in my anger,
  in my situation:
colored,
a girl,
& not rich

—NASRA VICTORIA ABDI, 18
  Somalia

WOMAN WARRIOR

i don't mind
    being weak for one day letting
the bigoted sexist see me cry
why would i say this
    after so many millennia?
    so much struggle?
    i am tired of trying to be a modern
matriarch
    sweating blood
    for all those who forget i won't
remind you
    let someone else let you run them
down
    i'm taking the day off
i'll be a woman warrior again
                                tomorrow

—J. VICTORIA SANDERS, 18
    New York

UNTIL IT'S OVER

I'm a sensitive soul
  old and wise
who looks at the world
through youthful eyes

Sheltered in the world
  I'm not of it
for I've not yet found
  a reason to love it

  A reporter I am
Recorder of my age
Drawing crisp pictures
with words on the page

That I write from pain
  is my greatest asset
Other people too have pain
Theirs and mine have met

They identify strongly
with my need to create
  God blessed/cursed us
with the very same fate

So I keep a pen in hand
  and say what I will
Paint pictures with words
And will keep on until
    it's over

—ADESINA ALEXANDER, 17
  New York

Motherlands and the Hood
Poems about Home and "Homelessness"

AFRICA

home
oh
home
the soul of your
variety
all of my bones
remember

—Lucille Clifton

HOMECOMING

Follow the lights, signs,
Tears, stories, adventures, and shame
To find your way home.

—EVA ABER ADOK OKWONGA, 16
  Uganda

MY HAITI

Listen. Listen to the soft pit patter of
the rain.
It tells a story.
Listen. Listen to the rush of the wind.
It sings a song.
Listen. Listen to the beating of my heart
It cries with grief.

Hear the rain.
It tells this story,
of a nation once abounded with pride,
of a nation once rich with gold,
of a nation once overflooded with the
rhythm of life,
of a nation vigorous in the realization
of hope.

Hear the wind.
It sings this song,
the revolution that pierced the veins of
those most brave,
the enslavement of those with ebony
skin,
the betrayal of family all in the name of
money,
the chanting of the voodoo priestess as
she calls forth a spirit.

Hear my heart.
It cries with this grief
Toussaint L'Ouverture who died a hero,
a liberator to be revered by many.
Dessalines, who championed the rights
of the oppressed.
Our sons and daughters, who died in
the struggle.
It cries for the deprived freedom it so
longed to taste.

"Mama will Haiti always stay this way,
will it not once again rise up and
be strong?"
"Hush child!"
"But Mama —"
"Hush child! Listen."
Listen. Listen.
The clouds wail.
They feel my grief.
The birds scream.
They hear my pain.

Haiti. Haiti.

Hear the rain.
It stops.
The story is done.
Hear the wind.
It calms.
The song is done.

Hear my heart.
It bursts.
Its pouch too small to carry my grief.

Haiti. Haiti.

—RACHEL AUGUSTIN, 15
  Haiti

CITY LIVIN'

Baby-sitters
Walks to school
Hopscotch in the Street

I Remember . . .

Cartoons and Kool-Aid
Streetlights and catfights and
Women Mama called "loose"

I Can Recall . . .

The friendly drunken bum
Waiting for the mailman to come
Brothers 'round the corner at the Carwash

My Dreams Haunt Me . . .

With the Beating of the girl next door
My Sister yellin' out the window,
"I'm not gonna take it anymore!"
and Daddy's Monkey on his back.

My Jones is my memory.
My memory is my addiction.
The streets are filled with intelligent
brothers gone wrong
and yesterday's favorite athletes.

Train Rides, Dead Ends
Gunshots, Bloodied Bricks
Everyone runnin' scared of the
Snatchman.

My memory only allows bittersweet
laughter about home.
Laughter that mellows my mind,
yet soothes my soul.

What I would be without my Jones
I don't know
So I'll wait for my next fix
to take me back to City Livin'.

—LESLEY TANAI SANDERS, 19
  New Jersey

WHERE MY BLOOD FLOWS DEEP

I come from a place where blood flows
deeper than the oceans
   Where the sun heals a tired soul
   While drums beat to rhythms in
motion.
   Oh, how I would love to return to
the land from whence I came.
To explore my natural heritage and
claim my rightful name.
   My journey would be so wonderful.
   My experiences so great
Lord, please help me to find my way
home, before it's too late.

—NAKEISHA ADAMS, 18
   Michigan

GROWING UP IN THE GHETTO

There's no place like the ghetto.
Hanging out in the front of my building
listening to rap music;
guys dressed in jeans
hanging off the side of their hips;
they sport big, flattop haircuts
and do the latest Hip-Hop moves;
or play basketball while
young girls jump double Dutch.

There's no place like the ghetto.
There, I know I am home
when I hear my music playing,
when I see names written in graffiti
in my neighborhood train station,
when I remember the corner store
where I used to buy five-cent candies
before going to school.

There's no place like the ghetto
where my people are full of pride
being the best dancer,
the best singer,
the best rapper,
the best dressed,
or simply
the most beautiful.

There's no place like the ghetto
where violence is common,

and the fear of guns
of drugs
of poverty
is part of many innocent lives.

There's no place like the ghetto
where the people struggle every day
and I can be me!

—TAISHA L. LEWIS, 15
  New York

CLOSER TO HOME

Listening to the sweet beat of reggae
music
Filling my soul
Warming my pulsing blood
Flashes of the evening sun
Red, warm
Hiding behind trees

You, sitting across from me
Bring back memories of my sweet home
Jamaica
Of summer parties, being in love, being
innocent and naive

And your warm innocent eyes
Soft radiant cheeks
Full, red lips
Remind me of home

There is so much of you that reminds
me of home
Of the hot sun, swaying palm trees,
pearly white sand and
blue sea
Bringing back more and more memories
And I draw a little closer
Hoping I can see more, feel more of
home.

—KAY WALKER, 19
    Jamaica

A MISSING SUN

I was born owning the rights of two
suns,
An American one draped in red, white
and blue.
Living only under this sun I have
longed
To hold and grasp the other.

I want to sip the African sun,
Each piece of golden hope melting
Inside my mouth.
I want the flavor to linger inside
Creating an explosion of ancestors
Who savored its rays the first century
of existence.

I want to bathe in its glory
With sounds of black feet piercing
The green, fertile land and drums
Coinciding with the thump of a
heartbeat.

I want to defy my native sun and drift
into
The relentless light of my African
bloodline.
Visit the calls and tongues of the skins
That have made my bones whole.

I want to journey to a light so strong
That the invisible chains will melt and
vanish
Into pools at my feet.

Take me to the sun
A sun I've never known
A sun I've only seen through betrayed,
Burnt eyes that hid
Behind the false chapters of history
books.
Let me embrace the new world with the
caramel skin
That has never slept in the cradle of
her beginnings.

—KIA HAYES, 17
  Pennsylvania

DÉRACINÉE*

I made it.
That trip across the Atlantic,
From Haiti to Zaire, barely conceived in
my mother's womb.
From Zaire to the United States in my
native shoes and
my luggage taped with stickers saying:
"I LOVE THE USA"

Dis-moi qui es-tu?
Who are you anyway?

Uprooted
is what Mummy calls me, saying,
"But, love, that is what you are in a
way."
In Zaire, my authentic name does not
exist.

Dis-moi de quel pays viens-tu?
Where are you from anyway?

I was born and raised in Zaire for 15
years
and my parents are Haitian . . .

Oh, you're one of those.

Now I live in America.
My Haitian compatriots ask,

"And you can't speak Creole?
Bad news. You are not really Haitian . . ."

I have made this long journey to
despair
and homelessness.
But my discovery of a new world
and the rebirth of a new generation,
the one taken between a rock and a
hard place,
awakens in me new feelings of adventure.

Mais, qui es-tu?
But who are you?

Uprooted.
I float on the Atlantic,
neither too close nor too far
from the African, Caribbean and
American shores.
Solitary, always. Lonely, never.
Because my God accepts me and is in
my company
everywhere.
Haitian and Zairean . . .
but human above all.

—MARIE-SABINE THOMAS, 21
   Haiti/Zaire

Déracinée is the French word for "uprooted."

TRIP TO MY SOUL

Poems that Reflect on Self and Spirit

from IF YOU WANT TO KNOW ME*

If you want to know me
come, bend over this soul of Africa....

—Noemia de Sousa

*This is an excerpt from a longer poem, If You Want to Know Me.

TRIP TO MY SOUL

The way I speak
    or the way I comb my hair
    The way I move
    or the shoes I choose to wear
    These outwardly things
    with your eyes you can see
    Take a trip to my soul
    and you will find me.

Where my seeds of dreams
    are planted in rows
    And they blossom freely
    like wildflowers grow.

Where the words I say
    dance in my mind
    To the rhythm of my heart
    and the bass of my soul
    Hear my song sound
    as its melody unfolds.

Where my closet of knowledge
    has a wardrobe of facts
    That hang up on hangers
    next to thoughts placed on racks.

Open the door of my spirit
    and take a step in
    Walk through hallways of emotions
    the corridors never end

View my channels of love
and the message they send
See the chandeliers of hope
    as
       they
         descend
From ceilings of faith
That are painted with devotion
Open the door of my spirit
View all my emotions.

Read a chapter in my book
   my story is told
   Take a moment in time.
   Take a trip to my soul.

—CHRISANDRA C. WELLS, 18
Nebraska

BLACK GIRL

"Yeah, girl, I slapped her.
You didn't really think
I'd let her trash about me and not do anything
About it, did you?
Girlfriend, puh-leeze.
I'm a Black girl, with a capital 'B'."

But what I didn't tell her
Is that all I can ever be
Is this oh-so-tough,
Don't-say-nothin'-about-me
Or-I'll-jack-you-up-strong
Black girl—
with a capital 'B'."
She don't know I can write poetry like nobody's business.
And God forbid that anyone
Ever see the hidden intellect beneath
The smooth Black girl facade.

"So, yeah girl!
She ain't ever gonna step to me again.
With her pathetic self!
I'm a Black girl with a capital 'B'."
I'm . . . a Black . . . girl . . . with a capital . . ."

—MALIKA HADLEY FREYDBERG, 15
New York

SELF-ESTEEM

Every morning I tell myself
I may not be as beautiful
And as smart as the other girls
But I will be somebody!

—MAYA LAWS, 13
   Washington, D.C.

REFLECTIONS

The outward appearance—an external
shell,
Emotionally different inside myself.

An alien reflection I project to others
Unwilling to express my true colors.

Afraid to let the real person show
For my true self—no one must know.

Inside me a soft little voice whispers for
recognition;
I bottled it—gave it no attention.

Wishing someday to shed this dreadful
skin,
Wishing for people to see what is really
within.

Wanting to change—to open my exterior
door,
Hoping for people to see my inner core.

—JASON DION BEASLEY, 15
Louisiana

I USED TO THINK

I used to think
white boys looked like girls
and white girls like
fairies.

And I stayed in the corner
of class to avoid them.
Miss Ann, the teacher, said I had a
problem,
and that Momma should take me,
a hollow-eyed,
big-boned brown gal
to see Mr. Charlie, the shrink.
He held up hideous black blurs
on cold white cardboards, which he
said were my dreams
or just the reflection
of what's wrong in the head
of every black child
who can't smile
the sambo grin
they wanted.

White folks have a tendency to strangle
the essence
in me.
And get rid of all the ain'ts and Ultra
Sheen
I brought each day to class
along with my Care Bears lunch box.

But Momma never cared enough
or forgot to pack my lunch
with something warm and brown
like the playground dirt I ate,
hungry for anything
the color of myself.

—JENNIFER MCLUNE, 18
  New York

THE QUESTION

You never asked about
my favorite color,
my first love,
the holes in my heart,
the state of my soul,
or the weight of your words upon me.

So how can you call me uppity?

You never asked me
what it's like to know the things I
know,
and live in this whiter skin,
and brush this straighter hair,
and feel the hate of your words upon
me.

So why should I think I'm "too good"?

And you never asked
about my place in this struggle,
my reason for fighting,
my tears, my shame
at the sound of those words:

"What are you?"

I am a walker of that painted line that
separates White from Black from Latina
from Native American; that separates
me from myself.

I am a daughter a fighter a writer a
singer a bringer of myself
to you and so many other things.

I am beautiful because of you.
I am beautiful in spite of you.
But we are most beautiful together,
filling our places in the spectrum,
listening to one another's stories,
and hearing
and healing
our lives in the telling.

—AMY E. AUZENNE, 19
   Texas

QUILTED SOUL

On happy days,
my hair is not nappy.
I have more than I owe,
and tomorrow I know
I will be building pyramids.

On sad days,
I remember
that my place in heaven is rented
and the currency demanded
is not the yen or dollar,
but my essence.

This will be
the prologue
to my death
unless I find the missing fabrics
of my soul
and weave them into a quilt
of my own design.

—SHERLEY JEAN-PIERRE, 19
   Haiti

TO 40-OZ. DRUNKS ON THE CORNER

When I strut 'cross the room with my
head shakin' lip-smackin' knee-slappin'
walk of mine
I know you see me.

When I slide on my slow
face-beamin' eye-gleamin' body-
screamin'
sexy smile of mine
I *know* you see me.

When I slip into my
pelvic-whirlin' finger-twirlin' toe-
curlin'
right-tight-out-of-sight dress
I know you see me.

But,
you best also see that I ain't no
kissed-ya dissed-ya not-gonna-miss-ya
sista,
So please
save the "Thank you, Ma'am"
for your Mama.

—MARIA GALATI, 18
    Wisconsin

LOVE RHYTHMS

Poems about Falling in Love and the Music it Brings

• •

COMMUNICATION

if music is the most universal language
just think of me as one whole note

if science has the most perfect language
picture me as MC2(AC1)

since mathematics can speak to the infinite
imagine me as 1 to the first power

what i mean is one day
i'm gonna grab your love
and you'll be
satisfied

—Nikki Giovanni

BABY, BABY

Baby, baby, come here
Let me whisper in your ear
Let me play the sax for you
 sing for you
Let me make you whistle
 like the wind
make your breath
 come and go
 like the ebb
  and flow
 of the tide
at high noon

—LYDIA OKUTORO, 21
  Nigeria

CRAIG

if i were to see you from a block away
i'd know you by your walk
i'd know it's you by your smile,
strains of dark black straight hair, and
baggy and sagging jeans with your
gangster lean
if i felt hands on my head
i'd know those were your hands
big, but with a gentle touch
with the smell of fresh cologne
if i heard a voice coming from a whisper
i'd know that they were your words
by the way they flow inside and out
like the sounds coming from
playing my alto sax

—JACLYN M. SMITH, 15
  North Carolina

I WANT ME A . . .

I want me a jazz-man
A cool, tall, dark man
Jazz Man, come blow on that horn for
me
While I sink into your soul silently
I want me a dancer-man
One of them strong, sensual, serious
men

Dancer-man, come groove for me
So you can melt me with your moves

Somebody bring me a gentleman
I want me a good man

—NATASHA DAVIS, 15
   Tennessee

MAURICE

You stumbled into my life
  without grace
  or charm;
  without wealth
  or experience;
  without hope
  or even luck.
But when you wavered,
  you slipped
  you tripped
and grabbed my hand
I laughed
and fell
    in love
with you.

—MARIA GALATI, 18
  Wisconsin

JUST LIKE YOUR KISS

I loved it when you kissed me today
just a sweet peck on the cheek
that melted on my blushing face
like cotton candy on
hot, sticky fingers
like butter on roasted pecans
simmering in a pan
evaporating like a drop from a
summer rain on the
scorching sidewalk
coming from nowhere
like a song remembered from long ago
like a funny thought that
made me laugh out loud
when nothing was funny.
Everybody stared at me
like I was crazy
like I was strange
like I was out of character,
like your kiss today
a sweet peck on the cheek
that melted on my blushing face
like cotton candy I lick off
hot, sticky fingers.

—ERIN CRANDALL, 18
   Alabama

PASSAGES OF DISCOVERY

rolling through paths of yesteryears
becoming tomorrow's tears
your hand is on my heart
forcing the flow of beats

catastrophes happen constantly
but you turn them into passages of
discovery,
remembering dreams
and dreams
and then
creating new ones
all I can say is "damn"
'cause I never knew
I could find you here
rapping me in your arms
as we
catch grooves
all the way to freedom

—RAIN ARRINGTON, 16
  Maryland

THE STRUGGLE CONTINUES

Poems about the Fight for Freedom

YOUT REBELS

a bran new breed of blacks
have now emerged,
leadin on the rough scene,
breakin away
takin the day . . .

young blood
yout rebels:
new shapes
shapin
new patterns
creatin new links
linkin
blood risin surely
carvin a new path,
movin forwud to freedom.

—Linton Kwesi Johnson

A BLACK GIRL TALKS OF THE UNITED STATES

See, they put me out of class today
because I questioned The
Establishment.
We were discussing the United States
and I said that the name "United
States" was hypocritical.
That made everyone uncomfortable,
and the teacher told me not to be
ridiculous.
"Our forefathers organized a union
where everyone has liberty and justice."
I said that was bull,
since there is a KKK and an NAACP
and a Nation of Islam
and organizations for Asians, Hispanics
and Native Americans, and every other
class of people
who are citizens.
And I said that if we were really united,
we would not need these organizations
or affirmative action, or quotas,
or minority scholarships, or welfare,
because we all would be equal,
and we would all get along,
and there would be no racial, social or
economic tensions,
and we all would be classified as
Americans,
not by our race, color, creed or ethnicity.
And the teacher asked me to be quiet,

but I kept on talking.
I talked about Slavery
and I talked about the Native
Americans
being cheated out of their land
and I talked about Indian Reservations
and I talked about the Civil War
and I talked about the Civil Rights
Movement
and I talked about Proposition 187
and I talked about Discrimination
and I talked about Hatred
and I talked about The Government
and I kept on talking.
And the teacher, well, she put me out
but that's okay
because we all know that I was right!

—WENDY IVY WILSON, 18
   North Carolina

LISTEN

These hands
have seen
so much more than they claim

ask me again
if it's my heart
or my mind
or maybe even my body
pulling me away,
and I won't tell

but
I can say
that neither
you nor I
have ever
tried
between screams
to listen
for the true sound of my voice

—RAIN ARRINGTON, 16
    Maryland

DESTINATION: FREEDOM

With determination in their hearts
And their feet set on the wonderful
path,
The path that would lead them to a
place
For which they had longed for years,
They stole away into the night
And did not look back.
They ran for days, weeks, months,
Just to find that place.
That place called freedom

—JENNIFER NICOLE ANDALL, 14
   Georgia

AFRICAN AMERICAN HISTORY

Four hundred years of oppression,
ruled by the whip and chain
torn away from my family,
my country and my name.

Inalienable rights were given back—
in 1863.
All men created equal?
All men except for me.

I had a dream almost destroyed
by a reality so contrary
but I vowed to live this dream
by any means necessary.

Now I'm still hated for what I am—
born of a dark-skinned mother.
It seems you will never realize
that black is just a color.

—RICHARD JOEL BOWERS, 19
Florida

FREEDOM

Martyr,
Freedom and rights
They're my God-given claims.
Could I die for a more noble
reason?

—NOREEN GLASGOW, 18
  Canada

SIBLINGS

My Brothers, my Brothers
What are we to do?
Am I paranoid or do we all not have a
clue?
Despite our plight we fight
                    each other
My Brother on my Brother

My Brothers, my Brothers
We smile at each other
But behind each other's back
We say the other's wack
And the depressing fact
is
the white man aint no saint
But neither are we

We can't afford to be divided
Our numbers are too few—even when
united
Our state of mind needs some revision
Because the man is quite happy with
our division
Don't you know?
they used to be scared of us
Cuz our people make more than just a fuss
or do we?
or can we? is it possible? Split

as
    we
        are

My Brother?
My Brother?
My blood is in you
As yours is in me
we are brothers—
But not a family

—MARTIN T. SUTLER, 18
  Washington, D.C.

CIVIL WAR

Greed blinds the bees, who
Scar themselves with war's hate, and
Split their precious combs.

—EVA ABER ADOK OKWONGA, 16
Uganda

AFTER TOMORROW

Poems about Hopes and Dreams of a Brighter Future

from STILL I RISE*

Just like moons and like suns,
With the certainty of tides,
Just like hope springing high,
Still I'll rise.

—Maya Angelou

*This is an excerpt from a longer poem, And Still I Rise.

AFRICA FINALLY UNITES

Down the street and up the alley,
I saw the children of Africa playing in
the valley,
Seeing the smiles on their faces, it was
so refreshing,
Black-on-black love were the bullets
they were shooting.

Redemption had finally come to them
all,
Welcome to Zion, was the sign written
on the wall,
Awake and lively, the children of Zion
displayed their gratitude,
On their knees in prayer to show that
God is really true.

It's a far cry from that twentieth-
century ghetto culture.
Oh how refreshing, Zion gave them an
exhilarating shower.
The blood, sweat and tears from all
those years,
Jah* had cleansed them and washed
away their fears.

Shouted the one from above, come and
cross the border,
Go back across the Middle Passage, he
ordered.

He that maketh wars to cease unto the
end of the earth,
Gave us everlasting life and forever
living which overcame the curse.

Peasants and servants alike lie together
in the field,
How so peacefully, how the river flows
so gently along the trees,
Likeness unto him, the children of
Africa possess his gentleness,
Through the blood and the bones, he
eradicates all of our weaknesses.

—SHELDON BRATHWAITE, 18
   Barbados

*_Jah_ is the word for "God" in Rastafarian religion.

MY PEOPLE, SLAVES NO MORE

I am a slave today
but someday I will fly away
Freedom I will be
and freedom will be me

To romp and roam the countryside
from no one will I have to hide
In this wide open country I'll be free
and in practically no time I decree
Definitely a slave no more
for these bonds of slavery I tore
To be finally a respected human being
but still the act of prejudice will sting

Free to travel, work and plow my land
Boy, this freedom thing is grand
Free to sing dance and play
On this plantation I'll no longer have to
stay
I will pray to my Lord oh God
Almighty
and hold on to my freedom tightly

For I will never be beaten again
by no man, even if I should sin
Boy, did I ever pray
that this would come about someday
The ties of oppression will no longer
fill my life
and neither will whippings or strife

I am a slave today
but someday I will fly away
Freedom I will be
and freedom will be me

—JASON D. CHURCHWELL, 13
   California

WHEN THINGS SEEM TO FALL APART

When things seem to fall apart
One after the other, and the goals you
dreamed of
Seem to slowly fade,
Do not dare let your spirit die,
Your soul to sleep,
Or your heart to weep
For things that are not yet done.

After tomorrow, pray for another day
To grasp again what's trying to slip away.

The point at which I stand seems to
move
Farther away from where I want to be.
But still I will dream and
I will become what I see.

Within me is a desire to learn of things
I do not yet know,
And to do things I have not done.
My single desire will lead me to where
I want to go.
I will no longer settle for mediocrity or
even good,
But will try to make excellence
From what is and is not yet understood.

—ALICIA INGRAM, 16
  Michigan

ETERNITY

Just for a second I glance away,
In that far-off direction;
   Where beautiful wind
   dances silently
Across ceaseless sands,
   serene skies,
   and stormy seas.

Just for a second I see
Without using my eyes;
   Where glimmering stars
   shine transparently
How long the sands have
   brushed the skies,
   nuzzled the seas,
   and I meet Eternity,
   Just for a second.

—CARINE MICHELLE WILLIAMS, 16
   Haiti

KNOWLEDGE

Sinking
   deep into the pages of my history
Reading of my people and how they
used to be.
Of Malcolm's rage and of Martin's pain,
Of murder, and rapes, lynchings;
Learning of a common aim.

A slow rising of anger and the descent
of tolerance,
A revolution too long awaited and a
hard road since.

A frustration that burned cities and
killed black men.
A unity of struggling against the white
man's sin.

I learned of the strong and proud
African race—driven
to defeat problems that were yet to be
faced.

With knowledge of my past,
I stand even taller before a world today
Possessing a power and a voice of yesterday.

—ALICIA INGRAM, 16
   Michigan

To Our Elders

Poems that Salute Ancestors, Elders, and Mentors

WINDOW MORNING

my ancestors
have claimed a storm
worn hollowed
tree
i am the wasteland
of our past
and at times
there is no air
yet i am a green bud

having broken
the earth womb
splitting the time
rooted trunk
of my beginning
my face
naked to God's sun

—Mwatabu S. Okantah

A TRIBUTE

This is for the brothas and sistas
who ain't here.
To those who have passed on
Their unfinished work to us.

For the stargazers,
The freedom lovers,
The peacemakers,
And my good friend Malcolm,
This one's for you.

This is for the brothas and sistas
who ain't here.
For the life givers
For the revolution makers,
The story writers,
And the rhythm shakers,
To you, I say, "Thank you."

This is for the brothas and sistas
who ain't here.
To you my beloved brothas and sistas
Who have not been given
Your respect due,
Rest in Peace.
Your work shall not be in vain.

—DONNA F. THOMAS, 19
  New Jersey

DADDY
(for E. G. Wilson)

Here I sit, the day of your death
Memories of you flood my heavy head.
Times when all a little girl had to do
was frown
To get what she wanted.
Spoiled like curdled milk,
I fester with disgust at the thought of
you gone.
What did they do to you
That made you leave us so soon?

—WENDY L. WILSON, 19
   New York

MESSAGE FROM A BLACK CHILD

I am a beautiful black child.
I am dark, I am light;
I can laugh, I can cry;
I can play and have lots of fun;

And I can learn
Because I have so much talent and
natural ability;
I can be anything I want to be.
I am strong.

I can be a doctor, a lawyer, an athlete,
an astronaut, a writer, a musician, a
businesswoman,
a scientist, an army general, or a leader
of my people.

Because in me I have the spirit of
Malcolm X, MLK Jr.,
Charles Drew, Paul Robeson, Queen
Nzingha, Michael Jordan,
Ronald McNair, Marcus Garvey, Julius
Nyerere, Langston Hughes,
Bill Cosby, Nat Turner, Hugh Masekela,
and Winnie and Nelson
Mandela.

I am from Jamaica, Philadelphia, Brazil,
Egypt, Nigeria, Cuba,
New York, Angola, Houston, Venezuela,

Sudan, Australia,
Panama, the Ivory Coast, and South
Africa.

But I can only achieve my full potential
with your help.
You must guide me, motivate me, teach
me, and push me to do
my best at whatever I attempt to do.

This is your responsibility as my
parents, teachers
and members of my community.
So that I will grow up to be a strong,
Beautiful Black Woman.

—AKILAH N. EVERING, 16
    Panama

MY INSPIRATION

(dedicated to Gwendolyn Brooks)

Gwen,
I love you
I love you because you are black and
proud of it
I love the way you bring magic to
words

Your voice,
    soft, whispering, powerful,
    calm, inspiring, telling,
    crying, singing, loving,
    glorifying and thanking.

Music!
Music, oh sweet music
Filling my soul,
    inspiring,
    reaching,
    teaching,
    healing,
Telling me I'm okay
I can make it
Telling me my color is magnificent
Telling me to be proud.

—KAY WALKER, 19
    Jamaica

TRUE MENTORS

I say the tears are in my eyes,
But I don't want to cry,
Some say it's all part of the great battle,
For our African prophets to be slain
like cattle.

You are in my memory still.
It was only yesterday that I was without
vigor and will,
A mixture of wolves and sheep were in
he meadow,
You gathered together the remnants and
showed me where to follow.

The future still seems so uncertain,
All I got to show for my actions is
none,
I'm forever blinded by the deep sleep,
For God's sake, your work I'll keep.

The words that you gave are still a
source of strength,
For vanity not, my head would not
bend,
Led so diligently by the truth of your
message,
Transformation from a frail youngster
to one of courage.

Praises to the Holy one and to you his
servants,
Through the rough seas, you all seemed
to manage the currents,
And although not totally free,
I praise thee who try to promote peace
and tranquillity.

—SHELDON BRATHWAITE, 18
  Barbados

ACKNOWLEDGMENTS

The scope of this volume made it occasionally difficult—despite sincere and sustained effort—to locate poets and/or their executors. The compiler and editor regret any omissions or errors. If you wish to contact the publisher, corrections will be made in subsequent printings. Permission to reprint copyrighted material is gratefully acknowledged to the following:

Nasra Victoria Abdi, for "jam with a poet & dancer," copyright © 1999 by Nasra Victoria Abdi. Printed by permission of the author.

Nakeisha Adams, for "Where My Blood Flows Deep," copyright © 1999 by Nakeisha Adams. Printed by permission of the author.

Adesina Alexander, for "Until It's Over," copyright © 1998 by Adesina Alexander. Printed by permission of the author.

Jennifer Nicole Andall, for "Destination: Freedom," copyright © 1999 by Jennifer Nicole Andall. Printed by permission of the author.

Maya Angelou, for excerpt from "Still I Rise," copyright © 1978 by Maya Angelou, from *And Still I Rise*, by Maya Angelou, published by Random House, Inc. throughout the World, except in the British Commonwealth excluding Canada, and by Virago Press in the British Commonwealth. Reprinted by permission of the publishers.

Rain Arrington, for "Listen" and "Passages of Discovery," copyright © 1999 by Rain Arrington. Printed by permission of the author.

Rachel Augustin, for "My Haiti," copyright © 1999 by Rachel Augustin. Printed by permission of the author.

Amy E. Auzenne, for "The Question," copyright © 1999 by Amy E. Auzenne. Printed by permission of the author.

ABOUT THE POETS

Nasra Victoria Abdi is originally from Somalia and currently lives in Ontario, Canada. Her poem *jam with a poet & dancer*, written when she was 18, addresses transition from an idealist state of mind to an acceptance of reality. For her, to be African allows her to boast a triple heritage, a gift she believes connects the body and soul to complete happiness.

Nakeisha Adams was born in Flint, Michigan, and currently lives in Southfield. She wrote her poem *Where My Blood Flows Deep* to signify what Africa means to her: home. Being of African descent has always been something she is proud of because it is a gift from her ancestors and God.

Adesina Alexander is a native of Brooklyn, New York, and is currently a student at Johnson C. Smith University in Charlotte, North Carolina. Her poem *Until It's Over* was written when she was an introverted 17-year-old. She is proud to be of African descent because African Americans have made tremendous contributions to the world. She relishes the knowledge that her ancestors survived the trials and tribulations of slavery, prejudice, discrimination, and segregation.

Jennifer Nicole Andall was born in New York, raised in New Jersey and now lives in Lawrenceville, Georgia. The inspiration for her poem *Destination: Freedom* came when she was 14 and studying slavery in school. The determination of those enslaved men and women makes Jennifer proud to be African American. Being of African descent means she can reach her goals because a long line of people made it possible.

Maya Angelou is one of the best known contemporary African American writers. She read her poem *On the Pulse of Morning* at President Clinton's inauguration in 1996, and received a Grammy Award for a recording of the poem in 1994. Her many books include her autobiographical series, beginning with *I Know Why the Caged Bird Sings*, as well as many books of poems, essays, and children's stories. She has also been a dancer, singer, actor, and producer. In 1992 she received the "Woman of the Year" award from *Essence* magazine. Some of her recent books are *Wouldn't Take Nothing For My Journey Now, A Brave and Startling Truth* and the children's book *Kofi and his Magic*.

Rain Arrington submitted her poems *Passages of Discovery* and *Listen* when she was 16. She is from Silver Spring, Maryland.

Rachel Augustin was born in Port-au-Prince, Haiti, and now resides in Uniondale, New York. *My Haiti*, written when she was 15, pays homage to her country of birth and her ancestors. Writing the poem was her way of keeping contact with her history. Being of African descent gives her pride not only in her African roots but also in the other groups that make up her Haitian history.

Amy E. Auzenne returned to her home in Houston, Texas, after graduating from Mount Holyoke College in Massachusetts. She wrote *The Question* at age 19 in response to an experience in which she felt obligated to prove her Blackness to some students who were not familiar with the Louisiana Creole culture. Amy is currently working on her first novel.

Jason Dion Beasley is from Baton Rouge, Louisiana. He wrote his poem *Reflections* when he was 15.

Richard Joel Bowers is a native of Stuart, Florida, who now lives in Willingboro, New Jersey. He wrote *African American History* at age 19 to address racist attitudes he witnessed as a high school student. For him, to be African American means that he carries centuries of wisdom in his blood and that he is a descendant of royalty.

Sheldon Brathwaite is originally from Barbados. He submitted his poems *Africa Finally Unites* and *True Mentors* when he was 18. He lives in Brooklyn, New York.

Khephra Burns is a writer and author of the books *Black Stars in Orbit* and *Mansa, Musa, Lion of Mali* (both from Harcourt Brace & Co.), and is co-author with his wife, Susan L. Taylor, of *Confirmation: The Spiritual Wisdom That Has Shaped Our Lives* (Anchor/Doubleday). He lives in New York City.

Jason D. Churchwell was born in Blythe, California, and now lives in Desert Hot Springs. He wrote his poem *My People, Slaves No More* at age 13 as a show of respect for his ancestors and their struggles. Being African American for him means having a proud history and being able to look at the past for strength for the future.

Lucille Clifton has been nominated twice for the Pulitzer Prize for poetry. She writes for both children and adults, and received the prestigious Coretta Scott King Award for *Everett Anderson's Good-bye*, one of her books for children. She has received fellowships from the National Endowment for the Arts and honorary degrees from the University of Maryland and Towson State University. Her recent books include *The Terrible Stories: Poems, Dear Creature: A Week of Poems for Young People and Their Teachers, The Book of Light*, and *Three Wishes*.

Erin Crandall resides in Mobile Alabama. She wrote *Just Like Your Kiss* when she was 18.

Natasha Davis wrote her poem *I Want Me a . . .* when she was 15. She is from Chattanooga, Tennessee.

Deborah Y. De Shong was born and raised in Brooklyn, New York, where she currently resides. *In Search of the Beat*, written when she was 18, is a tribute to the African American brothers and sisters who maintained hope while striving for positive possibilities for the future. As an African American woman of Caribbean descent she is proud of a rich, diverse culture that has taught her to persevere. Being of African descent means that she must constantly move forward and build on the legacy that has been paved for her. Deborah is currently pursuing a Master's degree at Hunter College in New York City.

Noemia de Sousa was born in Mozambique and attended secondary school in Brazil. She worked as a journalist in Mozambique, and lived for several years in Lisbon, Portugal, until she was forced to leave the country because of her out-spoken protests against the government. She moved to France and continued to write under the pseudonym Vera Micaia. Her poetry has been included in many anthologies.

Alexis De Veaux, a native of New York City, is a poet, play-wright, journalist, and fiction writer. Her books include *An Enchanted Hair Tale, Na-ni, Spirits In the Street,* and *Don't Explain: A Song of Billie Holiday,* as well as *The Dread Sisters,* an independently-published comic book.

Akilah N. Evering, originally from Panama, resides in Missouri City, Texas. She also lived in Zimbabwe for three years. Her poem *Message From a Black Child* was written when she was 16.

Maria Galati, from Wisconsin, wrote her poems *Maurice, Nappy Head,* and, *To 40-oz. Drunks on the Corner* when she was 18.

Nikki Giovanni was born in Tennessee, but moved to Cincinnati, Ohio with her family when she was two months old. She published her first poetry collection, *Black Feeling, Black Talk, Black Judgment,* in 1970, and has published more than thirty-five books, including poetry, an autobiography, and several books for children. She has received the Omega Psi Phi Award and has been given the keys to the cities of New York, Miami, and Los Angeles. Some of her recent books are *Love Poems, Racism 101,* and two books for young readers, *The Sun Is So Quiet* and *Shimmy Shimmy Shimmy Like My Sister Kate: Looking at the Harlem Renaissance Through Poems.*

Noreen Glasgow is from Toronto, Canada, and currently lives in Brampton. A student at the University of Windsor, she wrote *Freedom* when she was 18. It was inspired by Langston Hughes' poetry, and she strives for his love for people of African descent in her poems and artwork. To be of African descent evokes for her a feeling of pride and passion, a respect for all of Africa's children and distant relatives.

Malika Hadley Freydberg submitted her poem *Black Girl* when she was 15. She is from Rochester, New York.

Kia Hayes, who is from Philadelphia, Pennsylvania, wrote *A Missing Sun* at age 17.

Langston Hughes is one of the greatest voices of the Harlem Renaissance, the remarkable flowering of African American literary and artistic talent between the first and second World Wars. Born in Missouri in 1902, Langston Hughes became a prolific and highly-praised writer, producing poetry, novels, plays, songs, anthologies, biographies, children's books, newspaper columns and two autobiographies. He often incorporated the rhythms and forms of blues and jazz music into his poetry, as well as the everyday cadence of African American speech. Some of his poetry collections are *The Weary Blues*, *The Dream Keeper and Other Poems*, *Shakespeare in Harlem*, *Montage of a Dream Deferred*, and *Ask Your Mama 12 Moods for Jazz*. Langston Hughes died in 1967.

Alicia Ingram resides in Southfield, Michigan, and is currently a sophomore at Michigan State University. Her poems *When Things Seem to Fall Apart* and *Knowledge*, written when she was 16, were an inspiration for herself and others to overcome obstacles and a reflection of what it means to her to be of African descent. Her courage, strength, and determination come from knowing of ancestors who have faced the worst of conditions and survived. Alicia plans to attend law school after she completes her undergraduate studies.

Zarinah James wrote *Mutt* at age 16 when she was a boarding school student at St. Paul's School in Concord, New Hampshire. She currently lives in Hialeah, Florida.

Sherley Jean-Pierre is originally from Haiti and now lives in Brooklyn, New York. She wrote *Quilted Soul* at age 19 as a way of remembering that knowledge of self is important in dealing with all challenges. Being of African descent is her cultural, historical and artistic point of origin where her unique voice as a writer takes shape.

Linton Kwesi Johnson has been called a "reggae poet." He was born in a small town in Jamaica, and went to attend secondary school at the University of London. His first collection of poetry, *Voices of the Living and the Dead,* was published in 1974, and his first record, *Dread Beat An' Blood* (also the title of his second poetry collection) was released in 1975. He tours internationally and his recordings are among the best-selling reggae albums in the world. His poetry collections include *Inglan Is a Bitch* and *Tings An' Times.*

Maya Laws, from Washington, D.C., wrote *Self-Esteem* at age 13 to get in touch with her inner self. Being of African descent means for her that she must be thankful and take advantage of the opportunities for which her ancestors struggled.

Taisha L. Lewis is originally from Brooklyn, New York, and is completing her studies at the University of Virginia. She attended boarding school in Concord, New Hampshire, and at age 15 she wrote *Growing Up in the Ghetto* as a form of solace because she missed her neighborhood. For her, being of African descent means strength and the ability to triumph over obstacles. She feels fulfilled to be part of a people full of pride, beauty and culture.

Jennifer McLune is from upstate New York, where she is attending Bard College. A recipient of numerous awards, McLune's work has appeared in various publications. She wrote *My First Love* and *I Used to Think* when she was 18.

Katrice L. Mines is originally from Sandusky, Ohio, and now lives in Kent. The inspiration behind her poem *My Black Self,* which she wrote at age 18, came from a class discussion on the negative connotations of the word "Black." She believes that "Black" is a mesh of all the beautiful spectrum of colors. Being of African descent means that she is a piece of every part of the world. Katrice is currently a senior at Kent State University.

Mwatabu S. Okantah was born in Orange, New Jersey. He is an internationally-known poet and teacher of Pan-African studies at Kent State University. His honors include being named an International Academy of Poets Fellow in 1981 and a Rotary International Group Study Exchange Fellow to Nigeria, West Africa, in 1988. Mr. Okantah is the author of *To Sing a Dark Song, Afreeka Brass, Collage, Legacy: for Martin & Malcolm,* and, most recently, an epic poem *Cheikh Anta Diop: Poem for the Living.*

Lydia Okutoro was born in Nigeria and raised in New York City. Her poems *Quiet Storm, Baby, Baby* and *Haikus for Sisters* were written between the ages of 18 and 21. She wrote the first poem as a way to communicate her part in the universal struggles of Black people everywhere. The title of this collection, *Quiet Storm,* is from that poem, which embodies what it means for Lydia to be an African in America: fighting and celebrating together.

Eva Aber Adok Okwonga is a native of Uganda, and currently resides in Middlesex, England. She wrote *Homecoming* and *Civil War* at age 16.

Kelley M. Page wrote *Halo* when she was 19.

J. Victoria Sanders wrote her poem *woman warrior* at age 18. She is from the Bronx in New York City.

Lesley Tanai Sanders wrote *City Livin'* at age 19. She currently lives in Silver Springs, Maryland.

Jaclyn M. Smith was born in South Boston, Virginia and now lives in Butner, North Carolina. Inspired by her first love, the poem *Craig* was written when she was 15. For her, being African American can be frustrating, yet she tries to be someone of whom her ancestors would be proud.

Rochelle N. Spencer is from Augusta, Georgia, and now lives in Atlanta. A student at Florida A&M University, she penned *I Write Poems* at age 17. In college she learned more about African dance, music, art and literature and realized that Blackness is as much a cultural phenomenon as it is a racial one. For her, being of African descent means being part of a legacy that is rich, enduring and full of joy.

Martin T. Sutler (formerly Todd V. Darden) is originally from Washington, D.C. and currently lives in New York. He wrote *Siblings* at age 18 when he saw one Black man beat up another. To him, being Black in America means being on guard constantly. He believes that a person cannot be at ease because anyone of any race, including Blacks themselves, will ultimately do or say something hurtful.

Donna F. Thomas wrote *A Tribute* at age 19. She is from Newark, New Jersey.

Marie-Sabine Thomas wrote *Déracinée* when she was 21.
Kay Walker, who is originally from Jamaica, wrote *Closer to Home* and *My Inspiration* when she was 19.

Chrisandra C. Wells, from Bellevue, Nebraska, wrote *Message to the Dark-Skinned in Denial* and *Trip to My Soul* at age 18.

Elizabeth G. Weston, from Whippany, New Jersey, attended boarding school in Concord, New Hampshire. *Mulatto Child*, written when she was 17, was inspired by her struggle to come to terms with, and pay tribute to, her multiracial heritage. Her African American heritage gives her a better understanding of the world and provides her with a sense of community wherever she goes. Elizabeth now teaches elementary school in Wellesley, Massachusetts.

Carine Michelle Williams, whose native home is Haiti, wrote *Eternity* when she was 16. She lives in Miami, Florida.

Wendy Ivy Wilson wrote her poem *A Black Girl Talks of the United States* when she was 16. She is from Halifax, North Carolina.

Wendy L. Wilson wrote *Daddy* when she was 19. She is from the Bronx in New York City.